THE JUPITER CHRONICLES

Book One

The Secret of

The Great Red Spot

Leonardo Ramirez

LEONARDOVERSE.COM

The Jupiter Chronicles: The Secret of the Great Red Spot

Written by Leonardo Ramirez
Cover Design by PoochieMars
Editor: Kevin Ramirez

Published by LeonardoVerse, Nashville, TN
Copyright © 2012 Leonardo Ramirez

leonardoverse.com

Printed in the United States of America September 2012

ISBN (13): 978-0615633336 (paperback)

ISBN (10): 0615633331

Library of Congress Control Number: 2012909740

LEONARDOVERSE.COM

Here's what people are saying about the new Steampunk Children's series, *The Jupiter Chronicles*.

"*Jupiter Chronicles* is a fast-paced adventure that introduces kids to the Jovian world. Fantastic steam punk imagery, memorable characters, and intrigue will leave readers wanting more!"

~Tammy Derr, Fairy Tales Bookstore, Nashville, TN

"Ramirez expertly captures the banter of two siblings as they struggle to save Jupiter from the evil emperor. In this fast-paced Steampunk adventure, he touches on the grief children experience over an absent parent and their feelings of helplessness. Ian and Callie find strength within themselves to overcome their fears and their differences to fight the real enemy."

~Ann Wilkes, Award-Winning Blogger and Owner of Science Fiction and Other ODDyseys

"*Jupiter Chronicles* is a captivating story which keeps you going with very intense action all the way throughout the book while lending itself to frank and open conversations about absent fathers."

~ Anne Rucker, Educator

"I sat down with a copy of *Jupiter Chronicles* not sure what to expect. From the first page I was impressed by the writing style and realistic approach to setting and development. The creation of the characters was and is incredible. Each distinctly individual personality is a reflection of one identifiable in life. From the curious nature of children to the protective nature of a parent and all of the   personalities around them, Mr. Ramirez demonstrates he has truly found his talent and voice with this incredibly well-crafted book. This is the kind of book that gets the imagination moving at any age, making it perfect for children.

Young and old alike should take a moment to truly enjoy *Jupiter Chronicles* and dive into this Steampunk Science Fiction world full of adventure and excitement. It would be an effort not to enjoy it."

~Catrina Taylor, Xarrok Recommends

"I found myself wondering what was going to happen next. Kids will love reading the Steampunk adventures of Ian and Callie."

~Richard Groves, Nolensville Public Library

Special Thanks

———◆———

My sweet wife, Kristen.
My brown-eyed girl, Mackenzy.

You are both the joy and strength of my life.
Thank you for making life fun and sharing and shaping
this wonderful journey.

Poochie Mars
A selfless friend is one who gives when no one will ever
know his real name. You are a good friend.

The Quint Family.
Thank you for believing not just with words but with
deeds.

Ann Wilkes and Stacey Aragon

And our cover models:
Austin Sullivan and Mackenzy Ramirez

Foreword

For some time, I had wanted to go back to writing children's books since I had done so before. I figured the best time to do that would be in between my *Haven of Dante* books, which are of the Young Adult genre. My wife (who is a school librarian) suggested that I work on something for young chapter readers. She felt that the world had enough wizards and zombies to keep the older ones busy for a while. One afternoon, as I sat in my favorite chair, I was scribbling away on the laptop, trying to come up with something new to write.

After some time had passed, I had come up with something that I felt I could develop when our nine-year old daughter came downstairs and plainly said, in her sweet voice, "Daddy, why don't you write a story about kids that rescue their dad on another planet?" I looked up at my wife and then back down at the work I had already begun. Then I looked up again and said, "That sounds better than what I was working on!"

I say this because when good idea comes your way, roll with it. You never know where it will come from. This one came out of the mouth of my babe and, while it may say my name on the cover, this book is from my family . . .

. . . to yours.

We hope that you will enjoy this simple flight of fancy. More importantly, we hope that as you read this, you will enjoy it together with your child and share a memory. Kids are the most honest and precious treasure from God. Never lose a moment with yours because there is **no** such thing as "making it up."

~*Leonardo Ramirez*

THE JUPITER CHRONICLES

BOOK ONE

THE SECRET OF

THE GREAT RED SPOT

Let freedom rise and evil fall.
May light that shines uncover all.
Though storms may rage in colored skies,
I will not fear, my King is nigh.

...The Book of Jupiter

I grew up in a broken home. My parents divorced when I was seven. This story is for the young and young at heart who have shared that experience and are searching for some kind of healing.

If this is you, just remember one thing and you'll be alright.

You are loved.

And for my Pop.

TABLE OF CONTENTS

1 The Telescope.. 5

2 Imagine a Window 13

3 The Portal 20

4 Dreams of Steam 25

5 The Doomslayers 33

6 Stinky Frank 41

7 Drifterdash 50

8 The Book of Worlds............................ 57

9 Skyrocket Juno.................................... 65

10 The Sinu... 71

11 The Great Red Spot 77

12 Battle for Jupiter................................ 82

13 Forgive and Forget............................. 91

14 A Place Called Home 95

Who was Nikola Tesla? 103

Weapons and Orbs 104

About the Author...107

Contributors. 109

1

The Telescope

"You know you want to," Callie teased.

Her brother, Ian, ignored her as he put together the toy gun he had taken apart. Disassembling his toys was his way of avoiding things he didn't want to talk about. Callie, however, was persistent and wouldn't stop pestering him until she had convinced him to see things her way.

"That telescope is truly amazing. Just because you're still mad at Dad doesn't mean you can't use it."

"You want to use it, go ahead," Ian replied. "You're the one who wants to so bad, anyway."

Callie opened up her journal and spoke out loud as she wrote.

Dear Journal,

My brother loves misery. He is hopeless. I think he's a toad.

Love, Callie

A voice came from behind.

"Don't you think that's a little harsh, Callie?"

Nine-year-old Callie and twelve-year-old Ian Castillo didn't hear their mom coming into Ian's room. Callie gasped as she turned around, while Ian kept working on his project.

"Are you hungry?" she asked.

"No," Ian replied, sadly.

Camilla walked over to Ian and brushed his hair away from his face.

"I'm sick of beans and rice," he added.

Camilla's shoulders sagged.

"It's all there is," she said as she looked down.

Callie pulled out her journal and once again spoke out loud as she wrote.

Dear Journal,

My brother hates beans and rice. I'll go catch some flies for him. He might like that.

Love, Callie

"Stop it!" he screamed, slamming his toy gun down on the table.

Camilla quickly moved between them.

"That's enough, you two."

She turned towards Ian and knelt down in front of him. As she did, Ian asked, "He's not coming is he?" Camilla stroked his face gently.

"Sweetheart, it's been five years. I don't think your father is coming." She gently lifted his chin. "Let's not spoil your birthday tomorrow, OK? I've already invited some of your friends. It'll be nice and simple, but we will most certainly have fun."

Ian could remember clear as a bell the last time he and his father, Peter, had climbed up on the rooftop to gaze at the stars. Ian was very scared of heights. He always climbed up first while Peter followed close behind. It had rained on that day, so the ladder was wet.

"Be careful, Ian," Peter had said with a strong voice.

Ian climbed slowly and gripped the ladder tighter with each step.

"I'm fine, Dad." But, just as he had said that, Ian slipped. He could feel the cool wind on his neck as he fell backwards.

A strong hand lifted him up by the collar.

"I've got you, son," Peter said. He pulled Ian up, so that he could grab the ladder and finish his climb. Ian was then able to reach the top and that's when he saw it.

"It's a telescope!" Ian shouted.

"That's right," Peter said. "Happy birthday, son."

Peter showed Ian how to use the telescope. They searched for stars and planets and called them out by name. He pointed the telescope to one in particular.

"That's Jupiter."

"Is that the one with the red spot on it?" Ian asked.

"Yes it is, Ian."

"What is that big, red spot?"

"Some say it's like a hurricane or close to it."

"Wow," Ian exclaimed. "It's really big."

"Yes it is. You can actually fit 100 planets the size of Earth inside of it."

"Wow," Ian gasped, as he shivered in the cold night. Peter picked up the blanket and wrapped it around his son to keep him warm.

They stayed up late that night looking for other stars and planets and Ian wondered aloud how many of them there were.

"More than the grains of sand on a beach," Peter had answered.

That was the last time he used his telescope. The next morning, on Ian's birthday, the kids woke up to the sound of their mother crying. She was explaining to the police that she had no idea what had happened to Peter, but that he would not have missed Ian's birthday for anything in this world. After Peter disappeared, Camilla had to sell their horse and carriage for food money and tried to provide as best she could. She worked long hours for Mr. Furlong's Bakery on 40th Street, right around the corner of the famous inventor, Mr. Nikola Tesla.

Thankfully, Camilla had taken the time to teach both Ian and Callie how to read. This meant that they were able to attend public school which was not the case for other children because there were not enough teachers for everyone. They were to be there exactly at 9 a.m. and could not be late for any reason.

Many of the young boys that Ian knew were taught by their fathers how to be carpenters or bread makers but this was not true for Ian since his father had been gone for so long.

The Castillo's had to learn to live on beans, rice and wear hand-me-downs.

This was especially hard for Ian. He had an occasional job sweeping chimneys, but it was for pennies per job. Callie, on the other hand, stayed upbeat. She was also a very curious young lady which sometimes got her into trouble.

2

IMAGINE A WINDOW

Camilla tried her best to keep their home tidy and clean but there was only so much she could do when the wood floor was rotting away. Ian's room had no windows. He slept on a wooden bed with only a flat board underneath him. That night as he laid there, Ian pulled his blanket up to his chin hoping it would keep him warm and safe from the outside world. Camilla had painted a large window on his wall with stars and planets inside of it.

If I fall asleep, I'll be sad when I wake up, he thought to himself. So he began to say the names of the planets out loud to stay awake.

"Mercury, Venus, Mars . . ."

"Jupiter," Camilla said as she came into his room. "And you're supposed to be asleep, young man."

Ian quickly turned over and covered his head with his blanket. "I'm asleep," Ian said.

"Right," Camilla added. "Make sure you stay that way." Just as she was walking out of Ian's room she heard a loud knock on the front door.

Bam, bam, bam!

Ian jumped up. Camilla quickly turned to Ian and said, "Stay here. Do not get up."

"But mom," Ian said.

"No buts! Stay here." And Camilla quickly rushed past Callie's door. Curious Callie peeked out of her bedroom door to see who could have been knocking this late in the evening. They could both hear the front door creak open.

"Mr. Crowley," Camilla said sharply. "You will not disturb my household this late in the evening. My children are already in bed, mind you!"

Mr. Charles Crowley was a very short round man with a pointy nose and a ragged face. His hands always shook when he spoke. "Miss Castillo, I wish to speak with you about a certain matter involving the rent."

Camilla interrupted him. "Mr. Crowley we already agreed that my extra hours at the bakery would be more than enough to give me the means to pay you rent on time. And for heaven's sake, it's not even late yet! And by the way, it's *Mrs.* Castillo."

Mr. Crowley shook even more as if knowing he was wrong to ask the question again. "Well, yes quite right madam but I'm simply looking out for your well-being. In these uncertain times one mustn't be too careless."

"Mr. Crowley," Camilla said. "Why are you really here?"

Mr. Crowley looked away as if ashamed. "I care for all of my tenants, Mrs. Castillo and in light of the fact that Mr. Castillo is not present I simply want to make sure that everything is in order. By the way, have you spoken to **Mr.** Castillo lately?"

Camilla grabbed the door to close it. "Good night, Mr. Crowley." And she slammed it shut. She quickly walked towards Ian and Callie's room to make sure that they did not hear what had just happened and they were asleep as they should be. She peeked into Ian's room. He was as she had left him, turned over with the blanket over his head.

Callie was snoring . . . loudly.

Mr. Crowley walked into his office that evening. He picked up a candle to light it when he heard a deep voice coming from the shadows.

"Do not light the candle," the eerie voice said. "Tell me what you've discovered."

Mr. Crowley shook as he put the candle down. "I don't think that she's heard from him."

The shadowy figure spoke again. "Are you sure?"

Mr. Crowley tried to hold his hands still as they shook even more. "Yes . . . quite sure."

The shadowy figure looked out the window and into the night sky. "You've served us well . . . Mr. Crowley."

Mr. Crowley took a step closer. "So is my debt taken care of like you promised?"

"Yes," the shadowy figure answered.

"You are safe for now."

Fact or Fiction?

The telescope was invented by a man named Hans Lipperhey in 1608. He was born in Wesel, Germany and was a spectacle-maker by trade. Galileo Galilei was the first person to use the telescope to look out into space. He also discovered the planet Jupiter.

3

THE PORTAL

While Ian was sound asleep, Callie was awakened by a cold draft that came in through the open window. She got up from bed to close it when she noticed them. The distant stars that danced elegantly in the sky and shined their light into her bedroom had called to her. She wondered what it would be like to live on one of them. What would the climate be like? Would there be air to breathe? What could she do for fun on another world? Could she still play Cup and Ball? Hopscotch? Could she make new friends? The questions seemed endless. It was then that she pulled out her journal once more.

Dear Journal,

If I can't go to the stars, maybe I can see one up close. I'm going to go explore.

Love, Callie

Callie thought she would prepare as if she was going on a long journey. She pulled out her favorite black jacket and a pair of slacks. *It might be chilly on another world*, she thought to herself. After putting on her boots, she strapped on her bag and placed her journal inside of it. As quiet as a mouse, she snuck into the kitchen and grabbed a chocolate bar and stuffed it inside of her bag. She hoped with all her might that Ian would not wake up as she quietly tip-toed up to the attic. She took a deep breath as she turned the rusty door handle.

Creak

She closed her eyes and bit her lip, hoping she hadn't woken anyone up. Very slowly, she opened the door the rest of the way until she saw it; the telescope that she had begged Ian to let her use so many times was hidden underneath a dusty drape. It was obvious that no one had been up in the attic in years. There were cobwebs everywhere, but this didn't bother adventurous Callie. As she approached the drape, a large spider on the wooden floor hurried out of her way. She walked closer and closer to the drape and her breathing grew faster and faster.

The wooden floor beneath her feet creaked with her every step.

Creak... creak

She did not think twice about going in. Her curiosity, as always, was stronger than her fear. She pulled the drape off in one quick swoop.

Dust went flying everywhere. Callie coughed into her sleeve, so that no one could hear. She noticed the odd symbol on the side of the telescope. It appeared to be in an ancient language. Slowly, she pointed the telescope out of the window and looked through the eyepiece. She backed up and took a second look. All she could see was black. She couldn't see anything. Not a flicker of light nor anything else.

What kind of telescope is this? Callie wondered as she moved away from it. She went around the front to make sure that there was no lens cap on it. She looked closer into the lens and noticed that the glass seemed to move like water. "Wow," she said under her breath.

Suddenly, the attic door flew open with a loud slam.

"Callie! What do you think you're doing?" Ian shouted.   "I told you not to touch that!"

Callie jumped. "Aah! You scared me!"

Ian angrily stomped towards Callie. The telescope started to hum. A second later, it shook. Smoke rushed out from the base of the telescope and the tripod legs collapsed. Ian stared at it in shock, while Callie smiled from ear to ear. The eyepiece then pointed itself towards Callie. A beam of light shot out from the eyepiece directly at Callie and a voice from the base spoke, in a deep voice.

Recognize Castillo, Callista 004

The eyepiece then turned to Ian and, after a beam of light enveloped him, the same voice stated:

Recognize Castillo, Ian 003
Portal enabled.

The voice spoke one last time.
Prepare for launch.

4

DREAMS OF STEAM

While pieces of metal clanked and shifted, the lens of the   telescope began to grind around as it grew larger and larger. The tripod legs arranged themselves into a chair large enough for Ian and Callie. Two copper plates stretched out underneath the chair until they formed what looked like metal wings. Plumes of smoke shot out from the sides as the tube shifted behind the chair, forming a rocket booster. The lens grew until it became a dome over the chair, but it did not close all the way. The whirls, clanking and smoke finally stopped when the machine rested in its final form. Callie looked over at her brother who stood with his mouth hanging open and his eyes wide.

"I think we're supposed to get in," Callie said, with a smile.

"I think you're crazy," Ian replied. "We should call Mom."

Callie grinned. "Chicken," she said.

She rushed towards the seat and noticed a leather helmet with goggles.

"Ooh, fashion!" she exclaimed, as she put it on. Ian darted towards his sister who was sitting down inside of the craft.

"Callie, wait!"

Ian jumped in and tried to pull her out, but he accidently bumped a lever that was by his leg and he fell into the seat. The two heard the robotic voice call out one more time.

3... 2... 1... Launch.

The ship blasted out through the attic window in a loud roar. Pieces of glass crashed to the floor as they darted towards the heavens. From the porthole of the flying steam-powered machine, they could see their house moving away from beneath them at lightning speed. They dashed into the night sky and climbed higher and higher. Soon, they could see their hometown, then their state, then their country. In the blink of an eye, they were over the Arctic Ocean and could see all of the continents on the planet until they finally zoomed away from Earth's atmosphere and into the dark reaches of space.

"I'm ready to go home now!" Ian screamed in fright.

"Woo hoo!" Callie screamed, as she threw her hands up in the air.

As they approached the moon, their ship let out a loud squeal from its nose. A portal opened up just in front of them. They went through the tunnel fast enough to shoot past the moon and, in no time, they were able to see the red deserts of Mars from a distance. Just as fast, they reached their destination and were right in front of a giant red spot of swirling wind and gas.

"Wow," Callie murmured, under her breath.

Ian sat back in his chair and could hear the voice of his father, loud and clear, in his mind.

That's Jupiter.

As their ship dove down into Jupiter's atmosphere, the winds pushed back like the waves of a violent ocean. An alert sounded and the computer voice chimed in.

Located... setting course.

The ship turned a sharp left. When the clouds cleared, the stunning surprise that followed would be one they would never forget.

Giant cities powered by steam floated gently in the Jovian sky with massive pipes and metal contraptions underneath them to keep them safe from falling to the oceans of liquid hydrogen below. From a distance, they could see the locals dashing through the air on steam-powered backpacks with giant bat wings. They saw a passenger train shaped like a massive whale with bellows of steam shooting out from its blowhole cruising across the sky and farther away, large propellers pushed a huge sailboat across the landscape.

"Whoa," Ian muttered.

"Outstanding," Callie said.

A large ship zipped across their bow and left a trail of steam behind it. A new, eerie voice came onto their communications channel. "Doomslayer 1201 to unidentified vessel, you are in violation of Jovian airspace. By order of Emperor Phobos, you are hereby commanded to follow us to the *Skyrocket Predator*. Acknowledge."

Ian panicked.

"What the…?"

He looked for something he could use to communicate with them. Callie spotted a microphone and picked it up.

"Here we go," she said calmly. "Um… Mr. Noodle Maker, I don't know who Mr. Hobo is, but we just got here and you could be a little nicer."

Callie looked over at Ian, who sat with a stone-cold glare on his face.

"You're a dweeb," he said flatly.

The voice came back on.

"Unidentified vessel, this is your final warning!"

Ian snatched the microphone away from Callie.

"Mr. Doom, we don't even know how we got here. We need help."

Callie pulled out her journal and spoke out loud as she wrote.

Dear Journal,

My brother is a toad and we just met a noodle maker.

Love, Callie

Ian turned to Callie.

"Really? Now?"

The ship that pursued them turned around.

"You've been warned," the voice said.

The vessel fired a steam-powered rocket with a long cable attached that latched onto the hull of Ian and Callie's ship. Instead of exploding, it clamped on and quickly opened up into a drill.

It penetrated the hull and had exposed wires that it quickly connected with.

"Tractor engaged," the voice said. "Unidentified vessel, we have control of your ship. We are in route to the *Skyrocket Predator*, where you will be held for interrogation."

Callie looked at Ian.

31

"See what you did?" she said. Ian sat still once again and gave Callie a cold stare.

"You're a dweeb," Ian said as he crossed his arms and shook his head.

5

THE DOOMSLAYERS

The Doomslayer scout vessel threw Ian and Callie's ship onto the massive Skyrocket and cut them loose. After tumbling and rolling on the deck, Ian and Callie's ship came to an abrupt stop.

"Are you OK?" asked Ian.

"Yeah, I think so." Callie rubbed her elbow.

It was then that they heard a clanking noise outside. Something large and metallic was walking towards them.

"Get up, Callie!" screamed Ian. "We've got to get out of here!"

They heard a tap, tap, tap on the window of their ship. Ian and Callie looked up. A large, copper-colored, metal man with moving parts working inside his body stood outside of the window. He had a helmet with metal plates of steel sticking up from his head like wings and red eyes. He held a large steam rifle that leaked smoke out of the back.

His moving parts whizzed and clanked as he approached the window.

"That must be a noodle maker," Callie whispered to Ian.

"I am Doomslayer 1201 and by order of the Emperor you are to exit the vehicle," the robot said, in a gruff, mechanical voice.

Ian and Callie looked at each other, wondering what to do next.

"Now!" ordered the Doomslayer.

Callie grabbed her bag and they both carefully got up and exited their ship. They quickly found themselves surrounded by hundreds of other Doomslayers, all armed with steam rifles. Ian and Callie weren't going anywhere.

"Stay where you are!" ordered the giant Doomslayer. "Or you will be exterminated."

Ian took a step back and held on to Callie, who looked up at him with a raised eyebrow.

"OK, OK we're not moving," he said, anxiously.

Another Doomslayer came running up from inside the belly of the ship. This one did not have a steam rifle or a gun, but instead, he carried a scanning device with dials, exposed wiring and a steaming exhaust pipe. The rest of the crew stood guard, just in case the visitors decided to do something unwise. The large, robotic Doomslayer placed the device close to Callie and the belts and dials sprang to life. As he moved towards Ian, the scanning machine once again detected the presence of someone they surely did not expect to see. Surprised, the Doomslayer turned to his commanding officer.

"The humans are the son and daughter of First Petros, sir."

Ian and Callie looked at each other, confused and full of questions.

Petros? Ian thought.

Who are they talking about? Callie asked herself.

The Doomslayer turned to those under his charge. "Bring them!"

The mechanical soldiers instantly obeyed and surrounded their two captives with their steam cannons and marched them to see the one who had sent the order to shoot them down... Emperor Phobos himself.

The *Skyrocket Predator* was a floating ship the size of a small city. The guns and cannons that were on either side of the massive ship were powered by steam and stood ready to strike a fatal blow to anyone who dared to challenge it. It had a palace as its command center towards the rear of the landing deck. The Emperor resided in the Royal Chamber, situated at the very top of the palace, so that he could look down at everything and everyone. Ian and Callie were marched up to the highly   decorated throne room and it was there they met their newfound enemy.

Emperor Phobos rose from his large chair and slowly walked down the gold stairs of his throne, his red and yellow robe flowing behind him. When he took off his hood, Ian and Callie gasped.

Emperor Phobos was a large lizard with frills on the sides of his head that looked like large, spiked fans. He had long fangs and claws that could easily cut through wood like paper.

"Yessss, at long lasssst," the Emperor spoke, in a raspy, reptilian voice. "The son and daughter of First Petros have come to claim their land, but alasssss, you are rather late to the party, as you humans like to sssay."

Ian shook as he turned away from Phobos' long, slithery tongue.

"We don't know who Petros is," he said.

Callie glared at the Emperor.

"And who or what are you anyway?" she asked.

Phobos stepped closer and stroked Callie's cheek. "Eew!" she said, angrily.

Phobos took two steps back, so that he could look down on them.

"I am Emperor Timor Phobos of Mars. Years ago, the Jovians ssssuffered fell into chaos when their King went missssing. We came to bring order and offered to take care of them and to keep them safe from outsiders… like you." Ian tried to pull closer to Callie to protect her.

"We're not supposed to be here," Ian said. "We just want to go home."

The Emperor took a step closer to Ian.

"I ssssee. This is very interessssssting. Sssso, you were not ssssumoned here?"

Ian looked up at Phobos. "No, sir, it was an accident. We don't know who Petros is. We just want to go home."

"Interesssting." Phobos stroked his chin. "Well then, the only way home is through the gamessss." Phobos motioned the guards. "Take them!" he ordered.

The guards took Ian and Callie away from the Emperor and marched them towards the unknown.

FACT OR FICTION?

The prison cells on Despera were the most unclean places in the universe. Only those who had committed the most terrible crimes were sent there but when Emperor Phobos conquered Jupiter, he sent those who spoke out for freedom to this dreadful place.

6

STINKY FRANK

A Doomslayer scout vessel delivered Ian and Callie to the floating prison of Despera, where all those who challenged the rule of Phobos ended up. They were marched through the dark, dingy corridors until they came to their prison cell. Callie cringed and moved closer to Ian as they entered their cell.

"It's all right, Callie. I'm here," Ian said, as he tried to   reassure his sister.

From the back of the cell, they could see two glowing, white eyes in the darkness.

"Ian!" Callie cried as she ran behind her older brother.

They immediately noticed a strong, awful smell filling the cell. Callie held her nose as she moved away from Ian.

"Eewww! Did you fart? I was standing right behind you! What did you do that for?"

Ian raised his hands.

"It wasn't me, twerp!" he shouted.

In the middle of their argument, they heard a metallic frrraaaaaaaaaap sound, accompanied by a hiss of smoke   shooting out from the darkness behind the glowing eyes.

"Oh, I'm so sorry. Sorry indeed," cried a robot that clumsily clanked his way out of the shadows.

This robot was much like all the other Doomslayers except that it was rusty and a bit filthy. "My name is – fraaaaap – Francisus Flatulus Ferdinand and I'm afraid my – frap, fraaaaap – insides are getting the best of me because I am simply so excited to see you both, yes indeed!"

Callie giggled.

"What did you say your name was?" she asked.

The rustic, friendly Doomslayer clanked even closer and held out his hand.

"Francis Flatulus Ferdinand, my dear. My master named me after he reprogrammed me. I will admit it takes some getting used to but I have grown quite fond of it."

Callie stepped closer.

"Callie, stay back!" Ian cried out. She paid him no attention.

"That's a weird name," she said, shaking his rusty hand. "And it's too long. How about Frank?"

As the clumsy robot shook her hand, he began to shake until... fraaaap! Callie squinted.

"Or maybe Stinky Frank," she added.

"My name shall be whatever the daughter of Petros wishes it to be!" the robot declared.

Ian stepped closer and asked, "Who is this Petros that we keep hearing about?"

Stinky Frank took a careful step closer before responding.

"Long ago, there lived a good leader named First Javir. His son, Petros, set out on a journey to learn more about our universe and settled on your planet. There, he took a wife and had children. But, Javir was suddenly killed by a mysterious attack that Petros knew nothing about. After he was found on Earth, he was kidnapped and brought here. First Petros is your father."

The children gasped.

"My father is here?" Callie asked.

Stinky Frank looked over at Callie.

"Why, yes, he is. Before he was captured, he reprogrammed me and sent me to Despera to wait for your arrival." Stinky Frank took a step back and looked from side to side before continuing. "You see... I've been here waiting for you for five of your years. Even the mighty Emperor Phobos does not know who my master is."

Ian moved closer to Stinky Frank and asked, "Who is Phobos?

"After First Javir died, Emperor Phobos came to Jupiter and presented himself as a friend wanting to help a planet with no ruler. He promised to take care of the inhabitants, the Jovians, until the day they questioned him for being too harsh. On that terrible day, freedom was taken away from the people of Jupiter and they were no longer allowed to think for themselves. He used the hydrogen in the atmosphere to power his steam weapons, the Doomslayer scout vessels and the *Skyrocket*

Predator. On that day, the Jovians lost their independence all because they trusted someone they didn't truly know."

Ian and Callie looked at each other, shocked by all that they had learned.

"But, now, you must stand ready! You are about to be taken to the Drifterdash games!"

Ian frowned.

"What does that mean?" he asked with narrowed eyes.

The robot put his hand on Ian's shoulder.

"Do not fret," he said. "I have a plan — fraaaaaaap."

The guards approached and took them away to a large stadium, just outside the massive prison walls. Hundreds of Doomslayer droids cheered for the games with thunderous clapping and feet stomping. The prisoners stood behind guarded, iron gates waiting to be used in the games as targets. Doomslayers flew about with steam-powered Fireflights fixed to their backs. Emperor Phobos walked up to the floating podium soaring high above the audience and introduced the game.

"I bid you welcome, my warriorssssss and Joviansssss alike! Ssee that I am a graceful ruler that I would allow the games to continue?"

The crowds cheered and chanted, "Phobos, Phobos, Phobos!" The emperor held up a beautiful gray round object. "Behold the Orb!"

Callie turned to the prisoner standing next to her. He was an older man in tattered rags. "Sir, what's an ogre?" she asked.

The gruff old man turned to her. "Don't you know what that is? And it's pronounced Orb! As in the Orb of Winds....one of the three orbs of Jupiter. With this orb a kind soul can calm a mighty wind...or an evil tyrant can command an entire planet," he said with a rasp in his voice. "An evil monster tyrant like Phobos," he added.

Callie shuttered as Phobos continued, "But, sssee, the king who abandoned you has sent his son and daughter to take the Orb of Winds from us and cast you back into darkness! Have I not brought you together as one?"

"Yes!" the crowd cheered.

"Have I not made everyone equal in my eyes and provided for your every need?" Phobos asked.

"Yes!" the crowd cried.

"Then, let no one stand in our way! Let the Drifterdash begin!"

Everyone cheered for the Emperor as floating Doomslayers kept their guns pointed at the crowd for "safety sake."

Fact

or Fiction?

Why Stinky Frank was named Francis Flatulous Ferdinand.

His first name comes from a famous Terran (that's a person who is from Earth) whom First Petros admired named, St. Francis of Assisi who said "Where there is charity and wisdom, there is neither fear nor   ignorance." His middle name comes from flatulence (which means he farts quite a bit).

His last name (Ferdinand) comes from the famous Terran Sea Explorer, Ferdinand Magellan, who sailed around the Earth. First Petros was quite the explorer himself.

7

DRIFTERDASH

As the crowds cheered, two Doomslayer guards brought Ian and Callie into the arena. They were led to a gear rack, where there were two steam-powered devices of some kind and two Fireflights. One of the guards instructed them in a very, raspy voice.

"These are the Coil Eruptors," he said, pointing to one of the strange devices. "They are hydrogen disruptors that strap to your arm and are designed to immobilize your enemy when they are tagged with the device. Your goal is to tag your opponents with the Coil Eruptor before they tag you."

Ian picked up his and examined it closely.

"What happens if they tag us?" he asked.

The Doomslayer then took a step away from them. "You will be exterminated," answered the steam-powered robot. "The time for the games is at hand."

They quickly put on the bulky wings and stood before the emperor's floating podium. Phobos addressed the crowd once more.

"And, to show that I am gracioussss, for each Doomslayer you tag, I will release a Jovian rebel!" The crowd booed and hissed at that idea, but the Emperor would have his way.

"Silence!" he ordered. Phobos pushed back his robe and raised his hands into the air. "Let the Drifterdash begin!"

Callie shot up into the air at the touch of a button to get a head start. To her surprise, wings shot out from behind each Doomslayer and each rocketed into the air with their prey in sight. Ian stayed behind, grabbed another Coil Eruptor and quickly took it apart. As he did this, he surprised even himself. He had tinkered with taking clocks and watches apart and building sailing ships never anything this complex. Callie did not notice what he was doing or what was happening.

"Ian, I need your help!" she cried out.

Ian ignored his sister's call for help and continued his work. Emperor Phobos motioned the Doomslayer guard to come closer and asked, "What isssss he up to?"

"Unknown, sire," he replied.

While Callie managed to tag one robot by dodging and weaving from the Doomslayers that hunted her, Ian came out of his trance. His work was done. He aimed his weapon at a fast approaching Doomslayer and fired. The Doomslayer exploded in mid-air.

"Callie!" Ian cried out. "Come closer!"

A Doomslayer was about to reach for Callie, but she quickly dove down through the clouds towards her brother. Ian quickly threw his new repulse gun at his sister who caught it. She quickly turned and fired at the Doomslayer behind her. The Doomslayer's steam rifle fell through the air and Callie managed to catch it. While Ian built another, Callie shot down every Doomslayer she could while in flight. When Ian finished, he shot up into the air and fired into Emperor Phobos' podium sending it crashing down into the arena. He then fired at the prison gates where Jovians were watching from the outside. The Jovians were set free and they gathered as many weapons as they could from the arena and began to take their freedom back from their captors. Ian and Callie flew away from the stadium when they spotted a lone Doomslayer racing towards them, ahead of all of the other Doomslayers. The lead attacker reached for his gun. Ian and Callie pointed their weapons at him. Before they could fire, the Doomslayer turned and began firing at his comrades. Ian and Callie began firing along with him and they were able to slow the attackers down. Ian and Callie would not let their guard down and they turned their weapons on what they thought could still mean them harm. The Doomslayer turned in mid-flight and cried, "Do not fire!" The Doomslayer began to shake until a loud inner rumbling erupted from within his metal body.

Fraaaaaap!

Every piece of his outer shell blew outwards and revealed the metal man's true identity.

"Stinky Frank!" the two exclaimed.

"Boy, are we happy to see you!" Callie added.

"And I am happy to see you, my young friends. Come, we must – fraaaaap – travel away from this place before more Doomslayers arrive!"

"Where are we going?" asked Ian.

"We are going to the Book of Worlds. There, we will find the secret to defeating the Emperor and freeing your father."

Ian's eyes widened.

"Where is my father?" he asked.

Stinky Frank looked concerned for Ian as he answered.

"He is being held prisoner by the winds of the Great Red Spot. Now quickly! We must leave! Now that the Emperor knows you are free, more Martian troops will surely be   summoned."

Ian, Callie and Stinky Frank flew off across the sky and through the reddish clouds of Jupiter to find the answers that they desperately needed.

Those answers could only be found in the Book of Worlds.

8

---◦◦---

THE BOOK OF WORLDS

Callie opened up her journal and spoke out loud as she wrote:

Dear Journal,

The Book of Worlds is not one book. It's a big round room with a bunch of floating books that make me dizzy. I might throw up on another planet.

Love, Callie

Ian looked at Stinky Frank, who was looking a bit concerned.

"You get used to it," he said, as he shrugged his shoulders.

Stinky Frank proceeded to walk through the chamber with Ian in tow and Callie not too far behind.

"So, what is this place?" Ian asked.

"Jovian history and that of the greater worlds surrounding Jupiter are contained within the pages of each book," Stinky Frank replied, pointing towards the floating books. Ian looked around.

"There are so many of them," he said.

"Yes, there are. There are the books of Ganymede and Metis. Then, there's Synnott, Adrastea and Amalthea." Stinky turned around. "Then you have Thebe, Galileo, Leda, Himalia, Lysithea, Elara, Ananke, Carme and Pasiphae and Sinope. There's even the Book of Callisto and Io, which you are named after. There is also Europa.

Each world has its own orb. Jupiter is the only planet with three orbs."

"Why do you have these books?" Ian asked.

Stinky Frank appeared surprised at this question. "To know yourself is to know where you've come from young friend. Without that knowledge you are doomed to repeat your mistakes!"

Ian walked up to one of the books as Stinky Frank continued.

"Within each book is written not only the history of that world, but the location of each orb."

Callie became curious and walked up to ask a question herself.

"I still don't know what an ogre is."

Stinky turned towards her.

"An orb, my dear, is the mechanism that contains the essence of that world. Should, by some catastrophe, one of our worlds be destroyed, we can use the orb to recreate it. That way, the Jovian civilization will always survive. Jupiter has three orbs: wind, water, and fire. All three bring balance to our planet. Emperor Phobos has taken the Orb of Winds and Jupiter must have all three orbs working together in harmony in order to contain its essence. Perhaps one of the other orbs can weaken the Orb of Winds. We must find out which one."

He stared intently at Ian.

"Which do you think?" Stinky Frank asked. Ian took a step back and thought out loud.

"Well, fire won't cancel out wind," he began. "The heat would only make the wind stronger, so I'm going to say, water."

Stinky turned to Callie.

"And, what say you, my young friend?"

The Book of Worlds

Callie placed her finger over her mouth.

"I bet if you throw a bucket of water on the wind, it'll make it heavy and slow it down," she said.

Stinky Frank smiled.

"Indeed, you are the son and daughter of Petros. Now, let's see where the Orb of Water may be found." Stinky Frank opened the pages of the Book of Jupiter. "It says here the Orb of Fire lies with the Fiegans. They are a secretive race that lives in our midst hidden within our red skies. To date, we have never seen one but we know they are here."

"What about the Orb of Water?" Callie asked.

"Hmm, let's see," Stinky Frank said. He kept looking until he found the clue they needed. He pointed to one passage.

Beneath the realm of orange scape,
the eye protects the Sinu fate.

61

"The orb is with the kingdom of the Sinu," Stinky Frank said. "That is where we must travel."

Stinky Frank closed the book.

"But first, we will need a ship," he said.

FACT OR FICTION?

The first steam-powered airship was built by

Jules Henri Giffard in 1852.

9

SKYROCKET JUNO

"Why do we need a ship?" Ian asked, as they rocketed through the air. Stinky Frank flew closer to Ian and Callie to explain.

"The closer you get to the center of the planet, the hotter it gets. There is an ocean of liquid hydrogen that we must travel through in order to reach the Orb of Water."

Callie pulled out her journal in mid-flight and spoke out loud as she wrote:

Dear Journal,

My brother asks too many questions.

Love, Callie

"Oh, whatever," Ian snapped. Stinky Frank interrupted.

"We are approaching Nebulara where your father's ship is hidden." The three flew into a gas cloud of green, purple and red vapors that made it hard to see.

"Are we there yet?" Callie cried out.

"Almost," Stinky answered. They cleared the haze and, then they saw their father's ship. On the side of the ship, they could see the same markings that were on the side of the telescope and right next to it was the name of the mighty vessel… *Skyrocket Juno.*

"She's huge!" Ian said, excitedly.

A computer voice activated as they boarded the ship.

Recognize Castillo, Callista 004.
Recognize Castillo, Ian 003. Welcome aboard.

They looked around at the beautiful walls made of shiny metal and screens that lit up when they walked by them, as if the ship itself knew them both.

"There are only 18 Skyrockets in the fleet, not counting the one that Phobos built. Each ship and pilot becomes of one mind. They learn to tell the needs and wants of their pilots."

When they sat down, the ship hummed and came alive.

"Because this one belongs to your father, it knows who you are."

Stinky took the pilot's seat and steered the ship out of the cloud. But, as soon as they emerged from Nebulara, the ship rocked.

"What was that?" Callie cried out.

"Take your seats, my young friends. The Doomslayers have found us!"

The sounds of rocket fire on the outside of the ship almost knocked Ian over before he could get to his seat. He quickly moved to help his sister to her seat.

"You OK, Callie?"

She was scared and breathing heavily. "Yeah, I think so."

"Hold on!" Stinky yelled, as he tried to move the ship away from the firefight.

Ian looked up at a small opening that housed what appeared to be a large steam gun. He looked down at his sister.

"Stay here," he said.

"Where are you going?" Callie asked, in a panic.

"Just stay there!" He quickly ran up the ladder to the opening and the massive steam gun came to life.

"OK, let's see what you've got," he murmured to himself.

Ian fired a volley at the Doomslayers, knocking them out of the sky, one by one. Callie looked up at Stinky.

"Is he getting them?" she asked.

"Yes," he replied. "He surely is."

"Yay!" Callie shouted.

Callie pulled out her journal and spoke out loud as she wrote.

Dear Journal,

Don't mess with my brother.

Love, Callie

The *Skyrocket Juno* ship swam away from the colorful fog and set sail for the liquid beings known as the Sinu.

10

THE SINU

As they travelled towards the center of the planet, the ship shook violently and Ian screamed, "Are . . . we . . . there . . . yet?"

Callie rolled her eyes. "Yes, we're there!" she shouted.

"Liar... no... we're... not!" Ian screamed back.

"Actually," Stinky chimed in. "We are – fraaaaap – here."

Ian and Callie stood up to look outside the window. They held on as the ship abruptly slowed and entered an area thick with liquid gas – so thick that it was like diving into Earth's ocean and all they could see through the window was deep-orange liquid surrounding their ship. Ian stepped closer to the window.

"I can't see anything," he said. "It's all… orange."

An eye as large as the window suddenly opened up right where Ian stood.

"Aaaah!" Ian screamed, as he took three steps back.

Callie ran to her chair and turned it around. Stinky Frank picked up a microphone.

"I bid you greetings, Lord Ricas of Sinu. I am a servant of the First Petros and I bring his offspring on a mission to save our world."

Every instrument on the ship began to shake and rattle. A deep voice echoed throughout the entire cabin.

"Do not bring your war to the Sinu, metal man. Offspring or not, the pressures of the deep will crush the vessel you travel in if you do not turn and leave this place."

Ian took a step closer.

"Lord Ricas," he began. "They have taken my father   prisoner and we have to find him. Please help us."

The ship shook violently.

"Silence!" Lord Ricas ordered. "We will play no part in your petty war. Leave us now."

Callie turned her chair back around and peeked under the arm. "It's already here," she said. The large eye turned towards Callie and stared. The eye then squinted, as if Lord Ricas had smiled on the inside.

"What do you require?" Lord Ricas asked.

Ian took another step forward.

"We need the Orb of Water. With it, we can fight Emperor Phobos, who has the Orb of Winds.

"Very well," Lord Ricas of the Sinu answered. "If not for the offspring of Petros, the orb would not be entrusted to you, metal man. Return it to us without delay that you may continue to serve First Petros with your existence."

Stinky Frank bowed his head.

"Yes, Lord Ricas. We will. Thank you."

The ship began to shake once again. The instruments on every control went haywire, while the microphone that they had used to communicate dropped to the floor in a loud clang. Callie held on to the armrests on her seat. Ian grabbed the back of his chair, while Stinky

Frank shook so violently that his head almost fell off.

"What's happening?" Callie screamed.

Stinky farted uncontrollably. A leak sprang from an air vent, then another from beneath the floor.

"Ian!" Callie cried out in fear.

Water began to gather in the middle of the command deck. Drop by drop and stream by stream, the water made its way to the center of the floor until it formed a sphere. Finally, the transformation completed. The shaking stopped. The massive eye looked down at the orb with great fondness.

"Behold, the Orb of Water. Guard it well. Bring her safely home," Lord Ricas commanded.

Callie stood up and walked over to the eye and placed her hand on the window.

"We will," she said with a calm voice.

The eye then closed and faded into the orange ocean. Ian grabbed the orb and placed it safely in a compartment by his chair. He sat down and looked over at Stinky Frank, who was already seated in the pilot's chair.

"Let's go," Ian ordered.

The *Skyrocket Juno*'s engines roared to life. She turned upwards towards the sky and headed for the Great Red Spot.

11

The Great Red Spot

As the *Juno* zoomed towards the Great Red Spot, Ian and Callie could see the great wall of wind that made up the outer barrier of the giant storm. Its sheer size was terrifying. Ian looked over at Stinky.

"Are we even going to be able to go through that?" he asked.

"Your father built this ship. Surely, he would have made it strong enough to penetrate any atmosphere."

"I hope so," Callie added.

The ship began to rattle. Stinky Frank looked over at Ian. "It is time," he said.

Ian walked over to the compartment and very carefully pulled out the Orb of Water. Callie moved to stand next to her brother, as he gently placed it on a stand. Clamps extended out of the compartment and held the orb in place. Ian then walked over to a console and pressed a button, opening a roof hatch that led outside. The stand began to raise the orb towards the opening.

"Here we go," said Callie.

Stinky Frank brought the ship to a position right up against the barrier to the Great Red Spot. The *Juno* began to shake, as the orb lit up and electricity shot out from inside. Ian and Callie sat down in their chairs and put their seat belts on. Rain clouds gathered around the ship and poured violently straight into the Great Red Spot. Ian and Callie unbuckled their seat belts and ran to the window to see what was happening. The mighty winds of the Great Red Spot began to slow and slow and slow until the winds stopped. The red gases disappeared and fell towards Jupiter like rain. When the last of the gases fell, all that remained was Emperor Phobos.

The *Skyrocket Predator* and the *Skyrocket Juno* now faced each other. An army of Doomslayers surrounded the *Juno*. Ian happened to notice a large rock floating just behind the *Predator*. Emperor Phobos' voice hissed out through the loudspeaker inside the *Juno*.

"Ssso, you've resurrected the *Juno*, I see. And you have   delivered the Orb of Water into my grassssp. For thissss, I am mossst grateful."

Stinky Frank knew they were in for a fight. He turned around to tell Ian and Callie to strap in. Just as he did, Ian shot out on his Fireflight through the hatch door and began firing on every Doomslayer they could. He pressed a button on his headset.

"Callie! Stinky! Can you hear me? That's got to be Dad up on that rock! You blast your way through while I sneak in!"

Callie looked over and saluted Ian.

"Copy that, big brother."

As the *Juno* and the *Predator* exchanged fire, Ian made a run for the prison pad where he hoped he could find his father. Phobos could see where he was going out of the corner of his eye and moved over to the weapons console.

"Oh, nooo, you don't," he said.

Phobos pressed a firing button. A missile shot out towards Ian, who tried to fly faster towards the prison pad. Just before he reached it . . .

The missile exploded. Someone shot it down. But... who? It wasn't the *Juno*. They were too busy blasting Doomslayers. The missile was destroyed, but Ian wasn't out of the woods, yet. The blast had sent Ian tumbling through the air uncontrollably. His Fireflight shut down just above the edge of the floating rock. Right before he fell over the edge, a strong hand grabbed his collar.

"I've got you, son," Peter said in a strong voice.

Ian looked up and his eyes filled with tears. Peter set him down on the rock. They stared at each other for a moment in disbelief.

"Dad," Ian began. "The Martians are going to invade if we don't stop them."

Peter smiled at his son.

"Then let's go get 'em."

12

BATTLE FOR JUPITER

The *Juno* flew towards the prison pad and, in one quick swoop, picked up Peter and Ian. As they boarded, Callie ran to her father.

"Daddy!" she shouted.

"I have missed you so much, my princess."

"I missed you too, Daddy."

Peter had to move quickly. The computer voice activated.

Recognize Castillo, Petros 001.

"I need to take the controls, sweetheart."

Peter ran towards the command deck and a chair emerged from the floor. It was quite large and had enough controls to steer the *Juno*. The ship turned hard right and chased the *Predator*, which was now headed out into space. Ian took a chair.

"Oh, no, you don't," he said.

The ships exchanged fire, but the *Juno* was badly hit.

"Francis, put that fire out!" ordered Peter.

Stinky Frank ran over to the console where the fire was and quickly put it out. The slithery voice of Emperor Phobos filled the cabin.

"You are but one ship, Jovian."

Just then, an entire fleet of Martian Warships emerged from behind the *Predator*.

"You stand no chance," declared Phobos.

The warships prepared to fire on the *Juno* when suddenly…

A slew of missiles shot up from Jupiter's atmosphere and, one by one, they exploded on the Martian Warships. Peter turned and looked out of the side window.

"Oh my," he muttered to himself.

Every warship in the Jovian fleet fired on the enemy   invaders, destroying them one by one. A massive vortex of water rose from the surface of Jupiter and engulfed one of the ships that had been hovering too close to the atmosphere.

"It's the Sinu!" Callie gasped.

At the same time, plumes of fire shot from the skies above Jupiter and came together in a giant orb of fire that floated above the planet like a small moon. Bolts of fire shot out from it and destroyed the remaining ships that were attempting to invade the skies of Jupiter.

"And the Fiegan Firelords," Peter added. "No wonder we've never seen one. They live in the sky."

Ian ran up to the gunner chair on the top part of the ship and Callie grabbed the gunner's chair below. Together, they fired away.

"Hold on!" Peter shouted.

Despite the help, the *Juno* continued to be hammered by steam weapons from the *Predator*.

Callie managed to get a shot at the *Predator's* cannon, destroying it. "Yeah!" she shouted.

Ian slowed them down by firing on and damaging the *Predator's* engines.

"Francis!" shouted Peter. "Deploy the tractor!"

Stinky pressed a button and a projectile shot out with a   cable attached to it. The projectile latched into the hull of the *Predator*.

"Stay here and keep the kids safe," Peter said.

He quickly grabbed a Fireflight and a helmet. Peter turned and looked at his children.

"Stay here."

Callie's brown eyes widened. "His name is Stinky Frank," she said. Peter smiled.

He opened the inner door and, after rushing through, quickly closed it behind him. He could see his worried children through the glass. Ian started walking towards Peter, and Callie stopped him. Peter looked into their eyes intently.

"I'll be right back," he said.

After opening the outer door, he raced towards the *Predator*. Ian and Callie looked at each other. Callie smiled. Ian turned towards Stinky Frank.

"Does this ship have an autopilot?"

"Why, yes. Yes, it does," Stinky answered slyly.

Peter shot his way through the hatch of the *Predator*, but was quickly cornered.

You will never leave this ship alive!" Emperor Phobos shouted.

Peter had no way out; he was surrounded. Unexpectedly, he heard a familiar voice.

"I have what you want, Phobos!"

Ian had followed Peter to the *Predator* and he now had the Orb of Water in his hand.

"No, Ian! What are you doing?"

"I lost my father once and I don't want to lose him again!" Ian shouted back. "Please take what you want and leave this world alone."

"You can't trust him to do what he says!"

But Ian ignored him and stood up to face Phobos, who had a smile on his lizard-like face.

"Ssso touching. You have made a wise choice, Jovian. Now, give me the orb and your father will live."

"Ian, no!" cried Peter.

Ian looked over at Peter.

"I've got you, Dad," he said with a gleam in his eye. He carefully handed Phobos the orb.

"With this orb, I can have even more control over…"

Emperor Phobos stopped for a moment.
"What is this?" he asked himself.

Phobos took a closer look. What he held was not the orb he needed. His frills spanned out and shook violently.

10… 9… 8…

The side door to the ship exploded and Callie emerged from the smoke, looking for her brother and dad.

"Come on! Let's go!" she yelled.

Callie, Ian and Peter flew away from the ship and, just as fast, they were back aboard the *Juno*, safe and sound.

Phobos squinted.
"It doesn't matter," he murmured.

3… 2… 1… 0

The *Predator* was suddenly engulfed in a fiery explosion. Callie pulled out her journal and spoke out loud as she wrote.

Dear Journal,

Mr. Hobo got a taste of his own medicine. And I got my daddy back.

Love, Callie

13

FORGIVE AND FORGET

The *Skyrocket Juno* travelled through space on a course for Earth and away from Jupiter. On board, Peter knelt down in front of Ian and Callie.

"I'm taking you back home, where you'll be safe with your Mom."

"What about you, Daddy?" Callie asked. "Are you staying with us?"

Peter put his hands on both of their shoulders.

"Ian... Callie, I want you to know more than anything that I love you with all of my heart. But, the reason why Phobos felt he could attack our world was because no one stood up to fight against him while I was on Earth. I wanted to marry your mother after visiting Earth, so I stayed. But, now I must go back, so that I can return the orbs and rebuild our world."

Peter got up and walked towards the console. He pressed a button and pulled out two rings.

"These are the Jupiter Rings, worn by those in our family. You will be able to see everything that happens on our planet through them and even imagine yourself being there in your dreams. I will never be too far away."

Their rings glowed as they put them on. Peter knelt down once more and looked them each in the eyes.

"What happened with me leaving was not your fault; remember that. It was mine. I'm the adult and your father, and what happened was my responsibility. Never blame yourselves or your mother. I hope that you'll forgive me for that."

Ian and Callie rushed towards Peter and hugged him as hard as they could.

"Ian?" Peter asked. "How did you rig that Coil Eruptor to go off when it did?"

Ian pulled out a coil from his pocket and showed it to Peter.

"Easy. I knew that if I pulled out the coil and set a timer, it would erupt."

Peter smiled proudly at his children.

"Keep it as a souvenir."

14

A Place Called Home

Camilla stood by her kitchen window, hoping for some sign that the police had come across a clue that would lead them to the whereabouts of her children. She missed them dearly and had cried every night as she prayed for their safe return. The sun was going down, so she walked over to the counter to get another candle to light. It was going to be another long, sleepless night. As she reached over to pick up the candle holder, she felt the floor beneath her feet start to shake. The shaking then turned to a steady rumble. Camilla grabbed the table and held on to it for dear life.

"What's happening?" she cried.

Suddenly, night became day inside of her kitchen. The light became so bright, she could barely see. Suddenly, her body flooded with relief when she realized what had happened.

They were home. They had just been out with their father. Camilla quickly ran outside, knowing what she would find.

"Ian! Callie!" she shouted, as she ran towards the light.

Ian and Callie came running into their mother's arms.

"Mom!" they both shouted.

They hugged each other as tightly as anyone had ever hugged before. Callie held Camilla's shoulders.

"Mommy, why didn't you tell us about Daddy?" Callie asked.

Camilla stroked their faces. "Oh, loves, your father has many enemies and I simply did not want any of them to find you here. If word got out of who he really is they would have come looking."

Camilla kissed them repeatedly on the head when she noticed another shadow walking towards her.

"Hello, Camilla," Peter said.

"Hello, Peter," Camilla answered.

Peter stood there for a moment. Camilla rushed towards Peter and hugged him. Peter hugged her as tight as he could.

Peter brushed her hair with his hand. "I can't stay . . . I'm sure the children can tell you about everything."

"I understand," Camilla said. She always understood.

Ian tugged at his father.

"I want to come with you, Dad."

Callie quickly walked towards Peter, as if agreeing with her older brother. Peter knelt down.

"Your mother is right. I have many enemies and you'll be safer here, as long as you don't bring too much attention to yourselves. Listen to your mother."

A tear rolled down Callie's face. Peter placed a hand on each of their shoulders and stood up. He then turned and walked into the light. Peter turned around to say goodbye one last time.

"We can still have summers and Christmas, right?" Peter shouted.

Camilla looked down at her children, who looked up at her with pleading eyes.

"Of course!" Camilla shouted back.

The *Skyrocket Juno* then took to the skies with a mighty roar, as Ian, Callie and Camilla watched. Ian reached into his pocket and poked his finger with the coil he had removed from the Coil Eruptor.

"Well, I've got a ring now, so I don't need this."

He tossed it to the ground. Camilla put her arms around her children and walked them inside.

"How about some Earth food?" she asked. "Like cookies and milk?"

"Yea!" they both exclaimed.

The next morning, a gentleman by the name of Mr. Nikola Tesla happened to be walking in front of the Castillo household and noticed an odd piece of coil on the ground. He picked it up and examined it.

"Hmm," he muttered to himself. "I think I'll take this home and take a closer look."

As Callie sat by the warm fire in their home, she opened up her journal and spoke out loud as she wrote.

Dear Journal,

It's so good to be home. My brother is not so bad, but he is still a toad.

Oh and by the way, that is how Steampunk started. I like it.

I think it's going to be fun.

Love, Callie

Next:

The Ice Orphan of Ganymede

Jupiter Facts

The great red spot on Jupiter is a storm that has been going on for over 300 years.

Jupiter's volume is large enough to contain 1,300 planets the size of Earth.

The Planet has over 60 known satellites (moons) but most of them are extremely small and faint.

You can fit 100 Earths into Jupiter's great red spot.

It takes 12 Earth years for Jupiter to complete an orbit around the sun.

Jupiter is covered by an ocean of hydrogen with a sludge-like consistency.

Jupiter has a ring just like Saturn and Uranus.

Jupiter has the biggest moon in the Solar System, Ganymede. It is even bigger than Mercury and Pluto.

Source: PlanetFacts.net

Who was Nikola Tesla?

Nikola Tesla was born in 1856 in Austria Smiljan, Lika, which was then part of the Austo-Hungarian Empire, region of Croatia.

He was an electrical engineer and a mechanical engineer.

He became an American citizen in 1891 and worked with Thomas Edison and later gave the world electro-magnetic power. It was around this time that the Industrial Revolution began.

He died in 1956.

Source: teslasociety.com/biography.htm

Weapons and Orbs

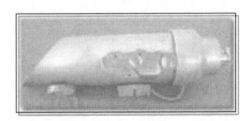

Coil Eruptors - hydrogen disruptors that strap to your arm designed to immobilize your enemy when they are tagged with a dart that shoots out from the device. These are primarily used in the Drifterdash games.

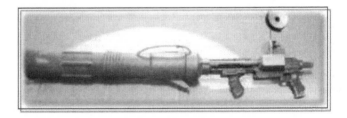

Steam Rifles - Used by the Doomslayers. Bulky and crude, these fire a hydrogen torpedo.

Repulse Gun – Reconstructed from the Coil Eruptor, this weapon fires an energy pulse that instantly dismantles machinery.

Orb of Winds

This orb is part of the "Jupiter Three" which can control the winds of Jupiter. The mighty wind surrounding the planet is what hides Jupiter from outsiders.

Orb of Fire

The heat that makes up the center of Jupiter is controlled by this orb. Without it, there would be no gravity. The Fiegan Firelords keep the Orb of Fire in their safekeeping. No one has ever seen a Firelord but they are described as massive creatures with eyes of fire that live in the skies of Jupiter.

Orb of Water

The liquid surface of Jupiter can be controlled with this orb. The Sinu have kept it safely in their realm for thousands of years.

About the Author

Leonardo Ramirez is a dad and husband first and then a writer. His greatest joy is spending time with family.

He loves comics! His first work published was a graphic novel called, *Haven*.

Leonardo is the author of a young adult series called *Haven of Dante* which is published through his self-publishing entity aptly named, Leonardoverse.

The writer is also a black belt in American Karate and enjoys teaching kids how to stay safe.

Visit Leonardoverse.com for more info and be sure to sign up for my blog.

Thanks!

~Leonardo

Contributors

Poochie Mars is the mysterious henchman of this work. He only comes out at night to work with the author on designing cover art or logos under a cover of darkness. No one has actually seen him but on occasion, when the sun rises in the east you can see his shadow race past the author's office door. In his wake, there can often be found a trail of banana peels, apple fritters and an occasional bacon and egg sandwich, which makes the author very happy and willing to clean up the mess he left behind.

Colleen Quint is a gifted art student who paints realism. Her artwork can be seen at colleenquintcreations.tumblr.com.

Ronan Hayes is a talented builder of Steampunk props. The devices he builds are all working models that come to life at the touch of a button. He often visits conventions and shows through his travelling mantra, Con-Artists.

LEONARDOVERSE.COM

To learn more about the author, visit his website!